I Am Brave

CANDIDE UWIZEYIMANA

Dedication

Remember, my young friend,
you have bravery within you, just like Mizero. Embrace new experiences, help others, and face your fears, be kind to others, honor others and what makes you unique to them. You, too, can be brave, bold, and make a difference in the world.

I Am
Brave

Once upon a time,
in a small friendly town,
there lived a child named
Mizero. Mizero loved
exploring and going on
exciting adventures.

He had a heart full of curiosity, and nothing scared him.

He may have been small,
but he was brave and bold.

Mizero had a special cape he wore every day. It transformed him into a fearless superhero ready to face any challenge.

With his cape billowing
in the wind, he knew he
could conquer anything
that came his way.

I Am
Brave

One sunny morning, Mizero noticed a tiny spider building its web on his windowsill.

Most kids would have been scared, but not Mizero. He carefully watched the spider spin its threads, admiring its hard work.

He didn't want to disturb it but knew it needed a new home.

Mizero gathered some leaves, twigs, and a small box to create a new home for the spider.

With patience and kindness, hye placed it near the window, making sure it was cozy and safe.

The spider crawled into its new home, looking grateful.

I Am
Brave

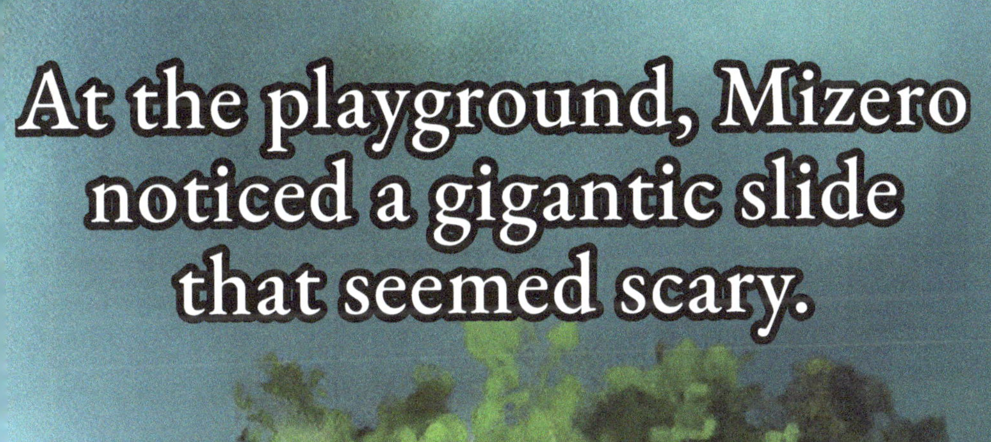

At the playground, Mizero
noticed a gigantic slide
that seemed scary.

Many children were too afraid to slide down it, but not Mizero. He climbed up the ladder, his heart racing, but he knew he had to be brave.

Taking a deep breath, he slid down the slide with a big smile on his face.

Mizero loved trying new things, so he decided to join a local soccer team.

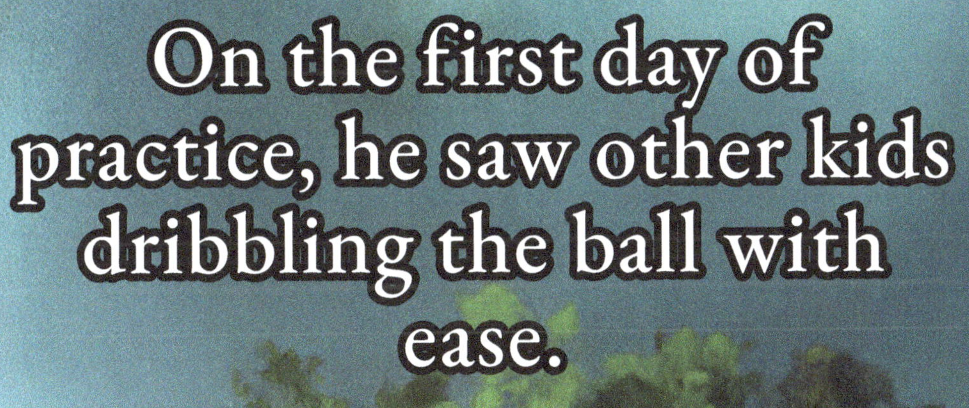

On the first day of
practice, he saw other kids
dribbling the ball with
ease.

Even though he struggled at first, Mizero didn't give up.

He practiced every day,
learning from his mistakes,
and soon became one of
the team's best players.

I Am
Brave

One day, Mizero found a beautiful bird with a hurt wing lying on the ground. He gently picked it up and brought it to his home.

He made a cozy nest for
the bird and took care of it
until it felt better.

It was a long process, but he kept going, showing kindness and bravery every day.

One stormy night, Mizero noticed a kitten getting drenched outside.

Without a second thought,
he grabbed an umbrella
and rushed outside to
rescue it.

He braved the hard dropping rain and skipped over the big puddles using his favorite rain boots, ensuring the kitten was safe and warm in his arms.

Mizero's bravery knew no bounds.

I Am
Brave

Mizero loved books, for they transported him to magical places and taught him new things.

He dreamt of adventures and believed that he, too, could make a difference in the world.

With every story he read, Mizero's bravery grew stronger.

I Am
Brave

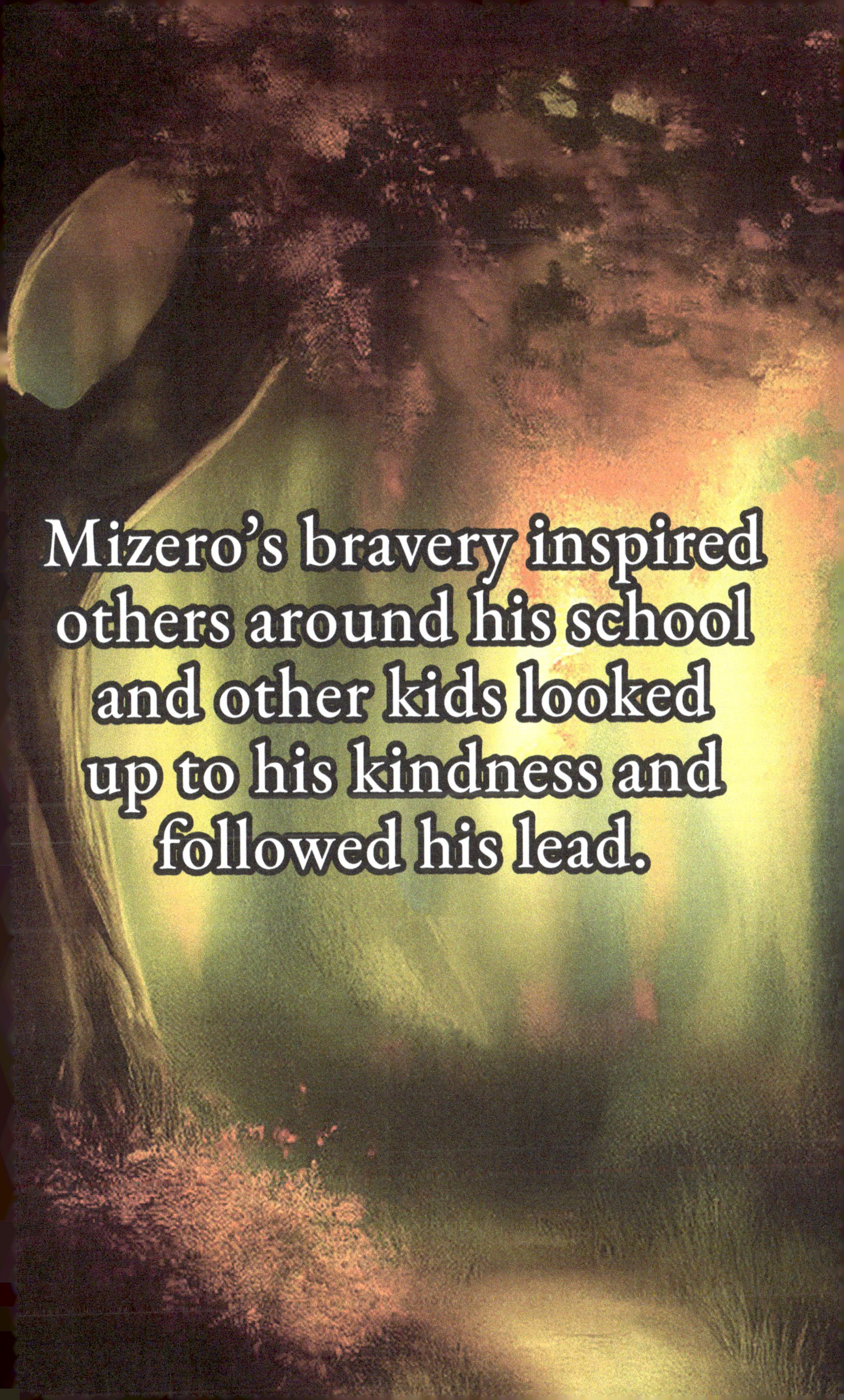

Mizero's bravery inspired others around his school and other kids looked up to his kindness and followed his lead.

Together, they formed a group of young adventurers, always ready to help others and face anything that came their way.

The End.